All about
POLAR BEARS

WRITTEN BY
Danny Christopher

Polar bears live
in the Arctic.

Polar bears are covered in thick fur.

Polar bears are
very big and powerful!

Polar bears can be dangerous to people.

Polar bears can
swim long distances.

Polar bears have a good sense of smell.

Polar bears hunt for seals on the ice.

Polar bears spend a lot
of time sleeping!